GW01403308

The Awakening

The Eternal Guardians, Volume 1

Tharun Vigneswar PS

Published by Tharun Vigneswar PS, 2024.

THE AWAKENING

First edition. December 15, 2024.

ISBN: 979-8227358288

Written by Tharun Vigneswar PS.

Table of Contents

Chapter 1: Ariana

Ariana Nguyen stared at the ceiling of her bedroom, wide awake despite the late hour. Her mind replayed the dream she had just woken from—she was running through a dense forest, the moonlight guiding her path as if she was a huntress on a mission. Every detail was vivid, from the scent of pine needles to the sensation of the wind against her skin. It was more than just a dream; it felt like a memory.

She glanced at her alarm clock: 3:12 AM. With a sigh, Ariana threw off her covers and sat up. She couldn't shake the feeling that the dream was trying to tell her something. Her feet hit the cold floor, and she padded over to her window. Pulling the curtains aside, she looked out at the quiet suburban street. Nothing out of the ordinary. Yet, something within her had changed.

As she returned to bed, her gaze fell on her bookshelf. Among the titles was a thick, leather-bound book that had appeared mysteriously on her desk a week ago. She had asked her parents if they had bought it, but they hadn't. None of her friends knew anything about it either. Ariana picked it up and ran her fingers over the cover. The book had no title, just an intricate design of a bow and arrow etched into the leather.

Curiosity piqued, she opened the book. Inside, the pages were filled with beautiful illustrations of ancient forests, wild animals, and a lone figure that looked eerily similar to the one she saw in her dreams. She flipped through the pages, stopping at an illustration of a huntress drawing a bow. Ariana felt a strange connection to the image, as if it was calling out to her.

She shook her head and closed the book. "It's just a dream," she muttered to herself. But deep down, she knew it was more than that.

The next day at school, Ariana tried to focus on her classes, but her mind kept drifting back to the dream and the book. During lunch, she sat with her best friends, Emily and Jason, who were engrossed in a debate about their upcoming science project.

"Ariana, are you even listening?" Emily's voice snapped her back to reality.

"Sorry, what did you say?" Ariana asked, feeling embarrassed.

Emily raised an eyebrow. "You've been acting weird lately. Is everything okay?"

Ariana hesitated. She wanted to tell her friends about the dreams and the book, but she feared they'd think she was crazy. "Yeah, I'm fine. Just didn't sleep well last night."

Jason leaned in. "Maybe you should try meditating or something. It helps clear your mind."

Ariana smiled weakly. "I'll give it a shot."

After school, Ariana headed to the track field for practice. Running had always been her way of escaping the stresses of life, but today felt different. As she stretched and warmed up, she couldn't shake the feeling that something significant was about to happen.

Coach Stevens blew the whistle, signaling the start of practice. Ariana took her place at the starting line, her heart pounding with anticipation. As she ran, the familiar rhythm of her feet hitting the track usually brought her peace, but today it felt like she was being pulled somewhere else.

Halfway through her sprint, a sudden burst of energy surged through her body. She felt an overwhelming urge to stretch out her arms. To her shock, a shimmering bow appeared in her left hand, and an arrow materialized in her right. Time seemed to slow down as she aimed and released the arrow. It flew straight and true, embedding itself in the ground at the far end of the field.

Ariana skidded to a halt, breathing heavily. The bow and arrow vanished as quickly as they had appeared, leaving her standing there, bewildered. Her teammates stared at her, eyes wide with shock.

"What the heck was that?" one of them exclaimed.

Coach Stevens hurried over, his face a mix of concern and disbelief. "Ariana, are you alright?"

She nodded slowly, though she felt anything but alright. "I... I don't know what happened."

Her coach sighed. "Take a break, Ariana. We'll talk later."

Ariana walked over to the bleachers, her mind racing. She had always been good at track, but this was something else entirely. She felt a connection to the bow and arrow, as if they were an extension of herself. She needed answers.

That evening, Ariana decided to return to the book. She flipped through the pages, searching for anything that might explain what had happened at the track. As she scanned the illustrations and text, one phrase stood out to her: "The Huntress Awakens."

She traced the words with her finger, feeling a strange warmth emanating from the page. "The Huntress Awakens," she repeated softly. It made sense now. She was the huntress in her dreams. The bow and arrow were part of her heritage, something ancient and powerful.

Ariana closed the book and leaned back in her chair. She wasn't just an ordinary teenager. She was the reincarnation of Artemis, the Greek goddess of the hunt and wilderness. The realization both thrilled and terrified her. What did it mean for her future? And what dangers awaited her as she embraced this newfound identity?

As she pondered these questions, a sense of resolve washed over her. She couldn't ignore the dreams or the powers any longer. It was time to embrace her destiny, whatever it might hold. Ariana glanced at the book one last time before turning off her light and climbing into bed. Tomorrow, she would start seeking the answers she needed.

Chapter 2: Rahul

Rahul Patel was running late, as usual. The vibrant colors of the early morning sun painted his bedroom walls in hues of orange and pink, but he barely noticed. His mind was preoccupied with the dreams he'd been having lately—dreams of epic battles and ancient wars. They felt so real, like fragments of a past life slipping into his consciousness.

He rushed through his morning routine, barely registering the taste of his cereal as he shoveled it into his mouth. His mother's voice called from downstairs, reminding him to hurry up or he'd miss the bus. With a quick goodbye and a hasty shove of his backpack, Rahul dashed out of the house.

At school, Rahul tried to focus on his classes, but his thoughts kept drifting back to the dreams. Each dream was more intense than the last, filled with vivid images of war and heroism. He saw himself wielding a sword, leading armies, and fighting fearsome creatures. It wasn't just the images; it was the feeling of command, the weight of responsibility, and the sense of honor.

During lunch, Rahul sat with his friends, Raj and Priya, in their usual spot under the large oak tree by the cafeteria. They were discussing their plans for the upcoming school festival when Rahul's phone buzzed with a notification.

"Hey, Rahul, what's up?" Raj asked, noticing his distracted demeanor.

Rahul glanced at the screen. It was a message from an unknown number, containing just one line: "The Sword of Destiny awaits you."

His heart raced. It was an odd message, but it resonated with the dreams he'd been having. Rahul tried to brush it off as a prank, but the message gnawed at him throughout the day.

As the final bell rang, signaling the end of the school day, Rahul couldn't shake the feeling that something significant was about to happen. He decided to visit the local library on his way home, hoping to find some answers.

The library was quiet and cool, a welcome relief from the hustle and bustle of school. Rahul walked through the aisles, scanning the titles of books on mythology and ancient history. He pulled out a few volumes that caught his eye and found a secluded corner to read.

Hours passed as Rahul poured over the books, searching for any mention of a "Sword of Destiny." Most of the texts were focused on various myths and legends, but nothing seemed to match his query. Frustrated, he was about to give up when a peculiar book fell off the shelf and landed at his feet.

The book was bound in dark leather with intricate gold patterns. It was titled "Legends of the Ancient Heroes." Rahul picked it up and opened it to the first page. The book seemed to be an old manuscript filled with detailed illustrations and stories of legendary heroes.

As he flipped through the pages, one particular image caught his attention—a detailed drawing of a sword with an inscription that read, "The Sword of Destiny, wielded by the great prince, Rama." The sword looked remarkably like the one he had seen in his dreams.

Rahul's hands trembled as he read the accompanying text. It described the sword as a powerful artifact with the ability to lead armies and vanquish evil. It was said to choose its wielder based on their heart and destiny. The description fit too perfectly with his dreams to be a coincidence.

His pulse quickened as he continued reading. The book detailed the legend of Rama, a prince who wielded the sword to defeat a formidable foe and restore peace. The more Rahul read, the more he felt a deep connection to the prince's story. It was as if the ancient hero's experiences were intertwined with his own.

Closing the book, Rahul felt a mix of excitement and anxiety. The dreams, the message, and now this book—all seemed to point to something significant. He couldn't ignore the feeling that he was destined for something greater.

As he left the library, Rahul made a decision. He would follow the clues from his dreams and the book to uncover the truth about the Sword of Destiny. He had to find out if he was truly the reincarnation of Rama and what that meant for his future.

The sun was setting as Rahul walked home, the evening sky painted in shades of pink and purple. He felt a renewed sense of purpose. Whatever lay ahead, he was ready to face it. He glanced back at the library, the book clutched tightly under his arm. The journey to understand his past and embrace his destiny had just begun.

Chapter 3: Nia

Nia Williams' life was usually quiet and predictable. Her days revolved around her studies, her passion for reading, and the occasional outing with friends. But the recent days had been anything but ordinary. Since her dreams began, her world seemed to tilt on its axis, revealing a reality she hadn't known existed.

It started with subtle signs: strange feelings of unease, a sense of being watched, and sudden bursts of energy. Last night's dream was the most vivid yet. Nia had been in an ancient temple, surrounded by towering statues and flickering torches. She had felt an overwhelming sense of duty and protection, like she was guarding something precious. When she woke up, she was disoriented, her heart pounding as if she had just come back from a real battle.

The next morning, Nia's mother gently knocked on her door, bringing her back to reality. "Nia, sweetie, time to get up. You don't want to be late for school."

Nia rubbed her eyes and reluctantly got out of bed. Her mother's concern about her recent behavior was evident, but Nia didn't know how to explain the dreams or the strange feelings to her. She had tried to brush it off as stress from school, but deep down, she knew it was more than that.

At school, Nia tried to concentrate on her classes, but the dreams weighed heavily on her mind. Her thoughts were interrupted when her history teacher, Mrs. Green, assigned a project on ancient civilizations.

Nia's interest was piqued. She had always been fascinated by history, especially ancient Egypt.

That afternoon, as Nia was researching for her project, she came across an old book in the library's history section. It was bound in faded gold and covered in intricate Egyptian hieroglyphs. The title read, "Guardians of the Ancient Realm."

Curious, Nia opened the book and began to read. The pages described the role of ancient Egyptian deities and their guardians. One chapter, in particular, stood out to her. It was about Nephthys, the goddess of protection and night, who was often depicted as a fierce guardian. The description of Nephthys resonated deeply with Nia. The goddess's qualities matched the protective instincts she had been feeling in her dreams.

The book mentioned that Nephthys was associated with guarding sacred places and ensuring the safety of the realm. As Nia read, she felt a strange sensation—a warmth spreading from the book to her. She could almost feel Nephthys's presence, as if the goddess was reaching out to her.

Suddenly, a sharp pain shot through Nia's head, and she gasped. The library around her seemed to blur, and for a moment, she saw flashes of ancient temples, dark figures, and intense battles. The vision passed as quickly as it came, leaving her breathless.

"Nia, are you okay?" A voice pulled her back to reality. It was Rachel, a classmate who had come to check on her.

"I'm fine," Nia said, forcing a smile. "Just a headache."

Rachel looked concerned but didn't press further. Nia closed the book and thanked Rachel before leaving the library. She walked home, her mind racing with the implications of what she had experienced.

Once at home, Nia decided to investigate further. She reached out to a local historian who specialized in Egyptian history and mythology. Dr. Alanis, the historian, agreed to meet with her after hearing about her interest and the strange occurrences she'd been experiencing.

The next day, Nia visited Dr. Alanis's office. The historian listened intently as Nia described her dreams and the sensations she felt when reading the book.

Dr. Alanis nodded thoughtfully. "It sounds like you're experiencing a connection to the goddess Nephthys. Sometimes, individuals with a deep connection to certain mythological figures can have these kinds of experiences."

Nia's eyes widened. "But why me? What does it mean?"

Dr. Alanis leaned forward. "It could mean that you are connected to Nephthys in a special way. Guardians often choose their protectors based on their qualities and their inner strength. You might be awakening to a role that has been part of your destiny."

The historian handed Nia a few texts on Nephthys and ancient Egyptian rituals. "These might help you understand more about the goddess and your connection to her."

Nia thanked Dr. Alanis and left the office with a renewed sense of purpose. She was starting to understand that her dreams and sensations were more than mere fantasies—they were part of her journey to embracing her true identity.

That evening, Nia sat in her room with the books spread out around her. As she read about Nephthys and her role as a protector, she felt a sense of clarity. Her instincts, her dreams, and her newfound connection were all pieces of a puzzle that was slowly coming together.

Nia's life was changing, and though it was daunting, she felt a growing sense of determination. She was no longer just a high school student—she was a guardian in her own right. The path ahead was uncertain, but she knew she had to follow it. As she closed the books and turned off her lights, Nia felt a profound sense of responsibility and readiness to face whatever lay ahead.

Chapter 4: Maya

M aya Singh had always been drawn to the night sky. As a child, she'd spent countless evenings gazing up at the stars, dreaming of distant galaxies and cosmic adventures. Her fascination with astronomy had only deepened over the years, leading her to pursue a degree in astrophysics.

This particular evening, Maya was working late in her observatory, analyzing data from a recent stargazing session. Her desk was cluttered with charts, star maps, and a computer displaying complex algorithms. The sky outside was clear, and the moon hung low, casting a silver glow over the landscape.

As she studied the data, Maya noticed an anomaly—a faint but persistent signal emanating from a distant part of the galaxy. It was unlike anything she had encountered before. The signal was rhythmic, almost like a heartbeat, and it seemed to be coming from an uncharted region of space.

Intrigued, Maya set up additional equipment to analyze the signal more closely. The rhythmic pulse was mesmerizing, and as she tuned the frequency, the signal grew stronger. It was as if the universe was trying to communicate something, but the message was still unclear.

Her fascination was interrupted by a sudden flicker on her computer screen. A new message appeared: "The stars align for those who seek." Maya frowned, puzzled by the cryptic message. It seemed to be linked to the signal but offered no clear explanation.

Determined to find out more, Maya cross-referenced the signal with historical astronomical records and ancient star charts. To her astonishment, she found similar patterns in ancient texts from various cultures, each describing celestial events and prophecies tied to the alignment of the stars.

One text, an ancient Sumerian manuscript, mentioned a celestial alignment that occurred once every millennium, said to herald the arrival of a chosen one who would wield the power of the stars. The description matched the signal's timing and rhythmic pulse.

Maya's curiosity was piqued. Could this be a sign of something significant? She decided to delve deeper into the Sumerian texts and related mythologies. The more she read, the more she felt a connection between the ancient prophecies and the signal she had discovered.

The following night, Maya conducted another observation, this time focusing on the region of space where the signal originated. She noticed a faint constellation that seemed to align perfectly with the rhythmic pulse of the signal. The constellation was unfamiliar, as if it had been hidden from view for centuries.

As Maya adjusted the telescope to focus on the constellation, she saw something extraordinary. A distant star began to flicker in a pattern that matched the rhythm of the signal. It was as if the star was responding to her presence, sending out a synchronized pulse of light.

Excited by her discovery, Maya documented her findings and prepared to share them with her colleagues. However, as she reviewed her notes, she felt a strange sense of urgency. The alignment of the stars and the message seemed to be guiding her toward a specific goal, but what was it?

That evening, Maya received an unexpected phone call from Dr. Rajesh Kumar, a renowned astrophysicist and mentor. He had heard about her findings and wanted to discuss them in person.

At their meeting, Maya explained the signal, the ancient texts, and the celestial alignment. Dr. Kumar listened intently and then revealed that he had been researching similar patterns for years. He believed that the alignment of the stars might indeed signal the awakening of an ancient power or knowledge.

"Maya," Dr. Kumar said, "this is more than just a scientific anomaly. It could be a key to understanding an ancient cosmic truth. You've uncovered something extraordinary, and we need to explore it further."

Determined to unravel the mystery, Maya and Dr. Kumar planned a series of observations and experiments to track the signal and its cosmic significance. They worked tirelessly, analyzing data and consulting ancient texts.

As Maya continued her research, she felt a growing sense of purpose. The stars and their ancient messages seemed to be guiding her toward a greater understanding of the universe and her place within it. She realized that her lifelong fascination with the night sky was leading her to a destiny far beyond her initial aspirations.

The journey ahead was uncertain, but Maya was ready to embrace the challenge. The stars had aligned, and she was prepared to uncover the secrets they held. As she gazed up at the night sky, she felt a deep connection to the cosmos and a sense of anticipation for the adventures that lay ahead.

Chapter 5: Ethan

Ethan Carter stood at the edge of his high school football field, the evening sun casting long shadows across the grass. The familiar roar of his classmates, gathered for a game, contrasted sharply with the turmoil brewing inside him. Ethan had always been a rebellious teenager, known for his fiery temper and unyielding sense of justice. But recently, something had changed—something he couldn't fully understand or control.

It all began a few months ago when Ethan started experiencing sudden bursts of electricity coursing through his body. At first, he thought it was stress or a trick of his imagination. But then came the dreams—intense visions of thunderous storms, mythical battles, and a powerful hammer that felt both foreign and familiar.

These dreams were more than just fantasies. They were fragments of his past life, revealing his true identity as the reincarnation of Thor, the Norse god of thunder. The revelation had come as a shock. On his eighteenth birthday, Ethan had discovered a hidden letter from his father, revealing their family's deep connection to Norse mythology and the true nature of Ethan's heritage.

The letter spoke of Stormbreaker, Thor's legendary hammer, and how Ethan was destined to wield its power. It explained that the divine lineage had been passed down through generations, waiting for the right moment to awaken. Ethan's temper and sense of justice, his struggles and his defiance, were all part of a larger plan. But with this knowledge came a heavy burden—a responsibility he wasn't sure he was ready to bear.

Tonight, he was supposed to be focusing on his senior year and preparing for college, but the weight of his newfound identity loomed over him. The chaos of the football game, the cheers of his friends, and the ordinary concerns of teenage life felt insignificant compared to the cosmic responsibilities awaiting him.

As the final whistle blew, signaling the end of the game, Ethan's friend, Jake, approached him, his face flushed with excitement. "Great game tonight, man! You were on fire!"

Ethan forced a smile, but the enthusiasm didn't reach his eyes. "Yeah, thanks. I'm just... tired."

Jake, noticing the change in Ethan's demeanor, gave him a concerned look. "You okay? You've been acting weird lately."

Ethan shrugged, not ready to share the truth. "Just got a lot on my mind. I'll be fine."

After Jake left, Ethan walked toward the bleachers, seeking solitude. He needed to clear his mind, to make sense of the conflicting emotions swirling inside him. As he sat alone, his thoughts drifted back to the dreams and the letter. He remembered the fiery storms and the hammer's immense power—how it called to him, urging him to embrace his destiny.

The night air grew cooler, and the first stars began to twinkle in the sky. Ethan's thoughts were interrupted by a sudden crack of lightning, followed by a rumble of thunder. He looked up, startled, and saw that the storm clouds were gathering overhead, forming a dramatic backdrop for his inner turmoil.

He felt a surge of energy, and the sensation was almost overwhelming. The sky seemed to respond to his emotions, with lightning flashing more intensely. It was as if the elements were reflecting his inner conflict.

Determined to find some answers, Ethan decided to visit the old family cabin in the woods, a place where he'd often gone to escape from the world. The cabin had been in his family for generations, a place where his ancestors had retreated to connect with their divine heritage. As he drove through the winding roads, the storm grew stronger, and the wind howled through the trees.

Reaching the cabin, Ethan entered and was greeted by the familiar scent of old wood and pine. The place felt both comforting and eerie, as if it held secrets waiting to be uncovered. He made his way to the basement, where his father had kept various artifacts and relics from their family's past.

Among the items was an old chest covered in dust. Ethan opened it and found a collection of ancient scrolls, runic symbols, and a leather-bound book. The book was adorned with Thor's hammer, Stormbreaker, on the cover. Ethan's heart raced as he opened it, revealing detailed illustrations and notes about his lineage, the hammer's power, and his role as Thor's reincarnation.

The book spoke of a journey—a quest to master his powers, to learn the true meaning of justice, and to wield Stormbreaker with wisdom and strength. The path ahead was fraught with challenges, but it was a path Ethan had to walk if he wanted to fulfill his destiny.

As Ethan read, the storm outside grew fiercer, the wind howling like a living entity. The power of the storm seemed to echo the awakening within him. He realized that he couldn't avoid his heritage any longer. It was time to confront his fears, embrace his true self, and learn to control the thunder within him.

With a newfound determination, Ethan closed the book and prepared for the journey ahead. The path to mastering his powers would be difficult, but he was ready to face it head-on. The storm outside was a reflection of the storm within, and Ethan was prepared to harness its power and find his place in the world—both as a teenager and as the reincarnation of a legendary god.

Chapter 6: The Awakening

The morning sun filtered through the trees as Ethan Carter prepared to embark on his journey. The ancient runestone he had discovered spoke of the Trial of the Thunder Gods, a series of tests designed to prove the worthiness of one who would wield the legendary Stormbreaker. The knowledge from the book and the visions from his dreams had given him a glimpse of what lay ahead, but he was determined to confront whatever challenges awaited him.

Ethan set out from the cabin with a sense of purpose. He followed the instructions from the book, which led him to a secluded forest clearing known for its ancient, mystical significance. The path was rugged and treacherous, winding through dense foliage and overgrown roots. The forest seemed to pulse with an energy that resonated with his own, making each step feel charged with anticipation.

The clearing was bathed in dappled sunlight, with ancient stones arranged in a circle at its center. Ethan could feel the power emanating from the stones, each one inscribed with runic symbols that matched those in the book. He approached the circle cautiously, his heart pounding with both excitement and anxiety.

The book's instructions guided him to stand at the center of the stone circle and begin the ritual. He took a deep breath and began reciting the ancient incantations from the book. As he spoke the words, the runes on the stones began to glow, and a low rumble of thunder echoed through the clearing, despite the clear sky above.

Ethan fought to maintain his balance as the storm raged around him. The power of the lightning seemed to challenge him, testing his resolve and strength. His hands trembled as he tried to control the swirling currents of energy. The thunder roared with a deafening ferocity, and the very air felt charged with electricity.

As he concentrated on the incantations, the storm's intensity began to wane. The lightning arced less violently, and the winds calmed slightly. Ethan's heart pounded in his chest, but he felt a strange sense of connection with the storm, as if the thunder and lightning were extensions of his own will.

He closed his eyes, letting the power flow through him, trying to visualize the calm eye of the storm amidst the chaos. He thought of his father's stories about Thor, the god of thunder, and how he wielded his power with both fury and control. The lessons he had learned from the book and his dreams guided him as he drew upon the legacy of his ancient self.

Gradually, the storm began to subside, and the blinding light receded. The once-chaotic lightning now danced in more controlled patterns around the stone circle, as if responding to Ethan's newfound command. He felt a surge of triumph and relief as the storm's energy became more harmonious and focused.

The thunder's roar transformed into a gentle rumble, and the winds died down to a soft breeze. The runes on the stones lost their intense glow but retained a subtle shimmer, signifying Ethan's success in the trial. The forest around him seemed to breathe a sigh of relief, the oppressive energy lifting as the storm subsided.

Ethan dropped to his knees, exhausted but exhilarated. He had completed the trial, proving his worthiness to wield the power of Stormbreaker. The storm had tested him, but he had emerged victorious, gaining control over the thunder and lightning that had once seemed so formidable.

As he gathered his strength, Ethan noticed a subtle change in the clearing. The stone circle now seemed to radiate a soft, welcoming light, and the air was filled with a sense of calm and accomplishment. He stood up, feeling a renewed sense of purpose. The trial had not only tested his control over the storm but had also deepened his understanding of his role and responsibilities.

Ethan's thoughts turned to his newfound allies, the other reincarnations of legendary heroes. He knew that his journey was far from over, and he would need their support and collaboration to face the ancient evil that threatened the world. The Trial of the Thunder Gods was just the beginning, and he was ready to embrace the challenges that lay ahead.

With a final glance at the now tranquil clearing, Ethan made his way back through the forest, determined to reunite with the others and share his experience. He was no longer just a rebellious teenager with a powerful legacy; he was now a guardian of thunder, ready to face the trials and triumphs of his extraordinary destiny.

Chapter 7: The Divine Vision

The night was still, and the moon cast a gentle light over the sleeping city. The five teenagers—Ariana, Rahul, Nia, Ethan, and Maya—had all drifted into a deep sleep, each one unaware that their dreams would soon intertwine in a way that would alter their paths.

In their separate dreams, they found themselves in a vast, ethereal realm where the boundaries of reality seemed to blur. It was a place of mist and glowing lights, with a sky filled with shimmering constellations and distant, echoing whispers. Each of them stood alone in this dreamscape, their surroundings seemingly familiar yet otherworldly.

Suddenly, a figure appeared before them. He was cloaked in radiant light, his presence commanding and serene. His form was majestic, his features noble and wise, with eyes that held the depth of ancient wisdom. He wore a robe that sparkled with stars, and his voice resonated like thunder, gentle yet powerful.

"Heroes of the Ages," the figure intoned, his voice echoing in the dreamscape. "I am Zeus, king of the gods, and I have guided you here for a purpose."

The teens felt a mix of awe and confusion. Ariana's eyes widened, her heart racing with the recognition of the divine presence. Rahul's posture stiffened, his natural leadership instincts coming to the forefront. Nia looked on with a blend of curiosity and apprehension, while Ethan's rebellious nature was tempered by a sense of reverence. Maya's warrior spirit was ignited by the sight of the god.

Zeus continued, "You have all been chosen for a great task. Your destinies are intertwined, and the time has come for you to unite. There is a place where your paths will converge, a sacred meeting point that will guide you towards your ultimate mission."

Ariana's dream vision shifted to show a map with a glowing point marked at its center. It was a location they had never seen before—a hidden sanctuary surrounded by dense forest and ancient ruins. The map was accompanied by a symbol, an intricate emblem that seemed to pulsate with divine energy.

Zeus's gaze was unwavering as he spoke. "This place is known as the Convergence of Fate. It is where your combined strengths will be tested and where you will receive guidance for the trials ahead. You must come together, for only in unity can you hope to overcome the darkness that threatens to engulf the world."

The dreamscape began to ripple and distort, as if the very fabric of reality was reacting to Zeus's words. The figure of the god grew fainter, his presence receding, but his message lingered in the dreamers' minds.

"Seek out the Convergence of Fate," Zeus's voice echoed one last time. "And remember, the strength of your bond will be the key to your success."

The dreamscape faded, and each of the five teenagers awoke in their respective beds, their minds racing with the same vision. They felt a strange sense of urgency, a calling that compelled them to seek out the location shown in their dreams.

As they rose and prepared for the day, the weight of their shared vision became clear. They were no longer just individuals with unique destinies; they were part of a greater plan, brought together by divine will. The Convergence of Fate was calling them, and they knew that their next steps would define their journey and their roles in the fight against the ancient evil.

Unbeknownst to each other, they each made their way towards the sacred meeting point, driven by the powerful dream that had united their destinies. They were about to embark on a journey that would not only test their individual abilities but also forge the bonds that would be crucial in the battles to come.

As they set out, the first rays of dawn lit their path, symbolizing the beginning of a new chapter in their extraordinary lives.

Chapter 8: The Convergence of Fate

The morning mist hung low over the forest as the sun began its ascent. Each of the five teenagers, guided by a shared, mysterious dream, ventured into the heart of the forest, drawn by an unseen force that promised answers. Their journey, though separate, was bound by a single celestial directive.

Ariana Nguyen was the first to arrive. She walked with purpose through the forest, the path illuminated by the soft light filtering through the trees. Her dreams had led her to this very spot, a clearing surrounded by ancient ruins. The sight of the weathered stones, covered in faded glyphs, was both awe-inspiring and reassuring. Ariana's senses tingled with anticipation. The familiar whisper of the forest seemed to guide her steps, drawing her towards the center of the clearing.

The forest floor was soft beneath Rahul Patel's feet as he emerged from the dense foliage. He was focused, his mind still buzzing with the divine vision from his dream. The sword at his side, a relic of his past life, felt heavy with purpose. As he approached the clearing, he saw Ariana standing amidst the ruins, her figure outlined against the backdrop of ancient stonework. He greeted her with a nod, a shared understanding in his eyes.

Nia Williams, following the call of the dream, approached the clearing with a cautious grace. The forest, usually a place of quiet reflection for her, now seemed alive with energy. Her protective instincts were heightened, her senses alert to every rustle and whisper. As she neared the clearing, she saw the figures of Ariana and Rahul already present. She moved forward, her quiet demeanor contrasting with the bustling energy of the place.

Ethan Carter arrived next, his presence marked by a burst of wind that stirred the leaves around him. The rebellious teenager had struggled to contain his restless energy, but the dream had given him a purpose. The thunderous power within him felt restless as he approached the clearing, his eyes catching sight of the others. He stepped forward with a mixture of determination and wariness, his gaze shifting between the familiar faces and the ancient ruins.

Maya Rodriguez, the final to arrive, emerged with the grace of a seasoned warrior. Her martial arts training had prepared her for many things, but the divine vision had brought her here, to this sacred place. As she entered the clearing, she saw the other four standing together, their presence forming a united front against the backdrop of the ancient ruins.

The five stood together in the clearing, their breaths visible in the cool morning air. The divine energy of the place seemed to pulse in sync with their heartbeats. They looked around, each sensing that the significance of this moment was profound. The ruins were adorned with symbols and runes that seemed to shimmer with a faint, otherworldly light.

As they waited, a figure began to materialize before them—a godly presence, ethereal and radiant. The figure took shape, a majestic deity with an aura of ancient power. The god's eyes, deep and wise, surveyed the group with a knowing gaze.

"Welcome, guardians," the deity's voice resonated through the clearing, rich and melodic. "You have been summoned here by the will of the cosmos. Your paths, though separate, have led you to this moment of convergence. The ancient evil you face threatens not only your world but the fabric of existence itself."

The deity's gaze shifted to each of them in turn, acknowledging their unique roles and strengths. "Each of you carries the essence of legendary heroes. Ariana, protector of nature. Rahul, the leader of valor. Nia, the shield of the innocent. Ethan, the thunderous force of justice. Maya, the warrior of honor. Together, you are the key to overcoming the darkness that approaches."

Ariana felt a surge of determination as the deity spoke. The forest around them seemed to hum with energy, reinforcing the gravity of their mission. Rahul's grip tightened around his sword, his resolve hardening as he absorbed the god's words. Nia stood quietly, her protective instincts sharpened by the divine presence. Ethan's restless energy seemed to focus, his anger now tempered by purpose. Maya, ever the warrior, felt a deep sense of responsibility settle over her.

The deity extended a hand, and a map unfurled in the air, its edges glowing with celestial light. "This map will guide you to the next phase of your journey. Follow it, and you will find the path to the heart of the ancient evil. But be warned, the trials ahead will test your unity, your strength, and your resolve."

As the godly figure began to fade, the clearing was enveloped in a soft, golden light. The five guardians exchanged glances, their faces reflecting a mixture of awe and determination. The task ahead was monumental, but they now understood that their shared destiny bound them together in a way that transcended their individual struggles.

With the map in hand and the deity's blessing fresh in their minds, the group prepared to set out on their new journey. They knew that their paths were now intertwined, and that the trials they would face would forge their bond into an unbreakable force against the ancient evil threatening their world.

As they left the clearing, the forest seemed to come alive around them, guiding them on their way. The journey was far from over, but the unity forged in the Convergence of Fate would be their greatest strength in the battles to come.

Chapter 9: The Path Unfolds

The mystical clearing buzzed with a sense of new beginnings as the group departed, the divine map clutched in their hands. The forest seemed to breathe with anticipation, and the rustling leaves felt like whispers of encouragement.

Ariana led the way, her gaze fixed on the map. "This way," she said, pointing to a glowing pathway that twisted through the trees. "We should follow this."

Rahul nodded, his expression focused. "We need to stay alert. The map isn't just guiding us; it's warning us of the challenges we'll face."

Nia, ever watchful, added, "I'll keep an eye out for anything unusual. The last thing we need is to walk into a trap."

Ethan paced restlessly behind them, his temper barely contained. "I hope this path isn't going to lead us into more trouble. I'm itching for a fight."

Maya, her martial instincts on high alert, glanced at Ethan. "We need to be strategic. Recklessness will only get us into trouble."

As they walked, the sun began to set, casting long shadows over the forest floor. They reached a small, secluded clearing perfect for camping. Ariana wasted no time setting up a fire.

"We'll rest here tonight," Ariana said, arranging the kindling. "We've had a long day, and we need to regroup."

Once the fire was crackling warmly, Rahul spread out the map on the ground. "We should review our route. The map is glowing more brightly in certain areas. That must mean something."

Nia sat beside Rahul, her eyes scanning the map. "These symbols... they look like they're pointing to potential hazards. We should be cautious."

Ethan, still restless, threw a stick into the fire. "I just want to get this over with. All this waiting is driving me crazy."

Maya joined them by the fire, her face serious. "I've been thinking about my past life as a warrior. The skills and sacrifices... I need to remember them. They might be crucial for our mission."

Ariana nodded. "We all have something from our past lives that will help us. We need to embrace it and use it."

Rahul, examining the map, looked up. "Tomorrow, we'll continue along the path. We need to be prepared for anything. I'll take the lead, but I need everyone's help."

"Count me in," Ethan said with a nod. "Just tell me where to strike."

Nia raised an eyebrow. "And I'll be watching for any signs of danger. We can't afford to be caught off guard."

Maya smiled slightly. "I'll make sure we're ready for whatever comes next. We've trained hard, and now it's time to put it all into practice."

As the night deepened, they shared stories and reflections around the fire. Ariana spoke softly, "I've been feeling more connected to nature lately. It's like the forest is guiding me."

Rahul replied thoughtfully, "It's not just the map. There's something more at play here. We're part of something bigger."

Nia, her voice steady, said, "I've been having strange dreams, too. They're not just dreams; they feel like messages."

Ethan grinned, his mood lighter. "Well, as long as we're all in this together, I'm ready to face whatever comes."

Maya looked around at her companions, her expression resolute. "We've come this far. We can't stop now. Let's make sure we're ready for whatever the future holds."

The night passed quietly, the forest a symphony of nocturnal sounds. As dawn broke, the group packed their belongings, each member feeling a renewed sense of purpose.

"We've got a long day ahead," Ariana said as they prepared to leave. "Let's stay sharp and keep moving."

Rahul rolled up the map and tucked it away. "Agreed. We need to make progress and stay on course."

Nia checked their supplies, making sure they were well-equipped. "Everything looks good. We're ready to go."

Ethan stretched, his earlier restlessness now replaced with determination. "I'm ready. Let's see what the map has in store for us."

Maya, her eyes scanning the path ahead, nodded. "We're stronger together. Let's face this journey head-on."

With that, the group set out again, following the glowing pathway laid out by the divine map. The forest around them seemed to shift and change, guiding their steps as they ventured deeper into the unknown.

Their journey was far from over, but they were united in their mission. As they walked, they knew that each challenge they faced would bring them closer together and closer to their ultimate goal: confronting the ancient evil that threatened their world.

The path ahead was uncertain, but with the strength of their bond and the guidance of the divine map, they were prepared to face whatever lay in their way.

Chapter 10: The Divine Revelation

The morning light filtered through the dense canopy of trees, casting dappled patterns on the forest floor. The group, invigorated by a restful night, continued along the glowing path. The map, now firmly in Rahul's grasp, pulsed with a gentle light, guiding their steps through the increasingly mysterious terrain.

Ariana, walking at the forefront, glanced back at her companions. "I've never seen a path like this before. It's as if the forest itself is alive and guiding us."

Rahul nodded, adjusting his grip on the map. "The map's light is shifting in intensity. It's as if it's reacting to something ahead. We need to stay alert."

Nia, her senses on high alert, scanned the surroundings with a wary eye. "There's an unusual stillness in the air. It feels like something is about to happen."

Ethan, who had been pacing restlessly, finally voiced his thoughts. "I'm getting a bad feeling about this. It's like the calm before a storm. Are we sure we're headed in the right direction?"

Maya, her eyes sharp and focused, reassured Ethan. "We've come this far. Trust the map and each other. We've faced challenges before, and we can face whatever comes next."

As they ventured deeper into the forest, the path grew narrower, flanked by towering trees with ancient, gnarled branches. The air grew cooler, and the light from the map cast eerie shadows on the ground. They walked in a tense silence, each lost in their thoughts.

The group emerged into a hidden glade, its beauty breathtakingly surreal. At the center of the glade stood an ancient stone altar, covered in intricate carvings that glowed with a soft, otherworldly light. The air around it crackled with an electric energy, and the ground beneath their feet seemed to hum with anticipation.

Ariana stopped in her tracks, her eyes wide with awe. "Look at that. It's like something out of a legend."

Rahul stepped forward, examining the altar closely. "This must be the place the map was leading us to. But what does it mean?"

Before anyone could respond, a shimmering figure materialized above the altar. The figure was tall and regal, with an aura of divine power. The figure's presence filled the glade with an overwhelming sense of peace and authority. It was as if time itself had paused in reverence.

The figure spoke, its voice resonating with a deep, melodic tone. "Welcome, guardians. I am Hermes, the messenger of the gods. You have proven yourselves worthy to receive my guidance."

Nia, awestruck, whispered to her companions, "It's Hermes... the messenger of the gods. This is incredible."

Hermes extended a hand, and a celestial map appeared in mid-air, glowing with a golden light. "This map will guide you further on your journey. It shows not just the path, but also the challenges you will face. Each challenge is a test of your strength and unity."

Ethan stepped forward, his curiosity piqued. "What kind of challenges are we talking about? And how do we overcome them?"

Hermes' eyes sparkled with wisdom. "Each challenge will test a different aspect of your abilities and your bond as a team. Trust in your skills and in each other. Remember, the greatest strength lies in unity."

Maya took a deep breath, her determination evident. "We're ready. We've faced hardships before, and we'll face whatever comes next together."

Hermes smiled, a warm, reassuring expression. "Very well. Your first challenge lies ahead. Follow the path on the map and prepare yourselves. The journey will be long and arduous, but it is through perseverance that you will find your true strength."

With a wave of his hand, Hermes vanished, leaving behind a lingering sense of hope and resolve. The celestial map faded from view, but the glowing path remained, more defined than before.

Ariana turned to her friends, her voice steady. "We have our first challenge. Let's make sure we're prepared. We need to stay focused and support each other."

Rahul nodded, rolling up the divine map. "Agreed. We need to strategize and be ready for whatever lies ahead. This is just the beginning."

Nia took a deep breath, her senses heightened. "I'll keep an eye out for any signs or omens. We need to stay vigilant."

Ethan clenched his fists, his determination burning brightly. "I'm ready. Let's show whatever challenges await that we're not to be underestimated."

Maya glanced around, her warrior instincts alert. "We've come this far, and we're not turning back now. Let's embrace this challenge and face it head-on."

As they set out once more, the forest seemed to welcome them, the path ahead illuminated with an encouraging glow. The challenges they would face were unknown, but with the divine guidance they had received, they felt a renewed sense of purpose.

The journey ahead promised to be filled with trials and revelations, but with each step, they grew closer as a team. Their bond strengthened by their shared experiences, they were prepared to face whatever challenges awaited them.

The forest closed in around them, the path winding through shadows and light. The ancient glade faded from view, but the memory of Hermes' guidance and the celestial map remained etched in their minds.

They knew that their journey was far from over, and the path to their destiny was only beginning to unfold.

With determination and unity, they pressed forward, ready to face the trials ahead and uncover the secrets of their true potential. The path to their ultimate goal lay ahead, and they were prepared to face it together, step by step.

Chapter 11: The Trial of the Beast

The labyrinth's exit opened into a dense, mist-shrouded forest. The mist curled around their legs like ghostly fingers as the group stepped cautiously into the clearing. Towering trees with ancient bark formed a protective barrier, and the soft rustling of leaves was the only sound breaking the oppressive silence. At the center of the clearing stood an archway, old and worn but inscribed with runes that glowed faintly in the dim light.

Ariana studied the runes with furrowed brows. The symbols seemed to shift and pulse, as though alive. "These markings... they seem to be part of the trial. We need to pass through this archway."

As soon as Ariana spoke, a deep, rumbling growl echoed through the forest. The sound was followed by the heavy thud of footsteps that seemed to come from all directions. From the shadows between the trees, a colossal beast emerged. It had dark, shimmering fur, eyes that glowed a fiery red, and claws that seemed to extend like deadly talons.

Ariana's heart raced. She quickly nocked an arrow, her fingers steady despite her pounding pulse. "Everyone, be on your guard! I'll engage it."

The beast roared, a sound that vibrated through the ground and made the air feel electrified. It charged at Ariana with frightening speed. She loosed her arrow, and it struck the beast's shoulder. It snarled and shrugged off the arrow as if it were a mere annoyance. The creature's eyes locked onto Ariana with a predatory glare.

Ethan, who had been observing the situation with growing concern, took a step forward. His hands crackled with energy as he prepared to intervene. "Ariana, get out of there! I'll distract it."

Ethan unleashed a bolt of lightning that struck the beast, temporarily stunning it. The beast roared again, shaking off the effects of the lightning and turning towards Ethan with a newfound fury. Maya, her sword drawn, moved in to assist. She slashed at the beast's flank, her movements precise and calculated. The blade cut through the beast's fur, drawing a howl of pain from the creature.

Rahul, feeling the weight of the divine weapon in his hand, took aim at the beast's heart. He focused intently, channeling his energy and summoning the divine power within him. The weapon glowed with a celestial light as he swung it with all his might. The strike landed with a resonant impact, but the beast, though visibly injured, continued to fight with relentless ferocity.

Nia, who had been standing back, used her protective abilities to shield her friends from the beast's wild swipes. Her hands glowed with a soft blue light as she erected a barrier around the group. Her eyes darted around, searching for any hidden threats or weaknesses in their adversary.

Despite their combined efforts, the beast proved to be an unyielding opponent. It adapted quickly to their attacks, its movements becoming more unpredictable and aggressive. The battle intensified as the beast's fury grew, forcing Ariana and her friends to push their abilities to the limit.

The clearing became a chaotic battlefield. Ariana ducked and rolled to avoid the beast's claws, firing arrows with precision. Ethan continued to use his lightning to create openings, but he had to be careful not to hit his allies. Maya danced around the beast, her sword flashing as she aimed for vulnerable spots. Rahul coordinated their efforts, directing the attacks and finding the right moments to strike. Nia maintained her barrier, her focus unwavering as she kept her friends safe.

Hours seemed to pass as they fought, the mist around them growing thicker with the sweat and breath of the battle. The beast's roars and the clash of their weapons created a symphony of chaos. Finally, with a coordinated strike, they managed to bring the beast to its knees. Ariana's final arrow struck true, and Rahul's divine weapon delivered the finishing blow.

Breathing heavily, Ariana surveyed the aftermath of the battle. The once-mighty beast lay defeated on the forest floor, its eyes closed in death. The group was exhausted but relieved.

"That was intense," Ariana said, wiping sweat from her brow. "But we did it. We passed the trial."

Rahul nodded, his eyes scanning the clearing for any more threats. "We need to stay alert. This was just one trial. There's more to come."

The ancient archway, now illuminated with a bright, welcoming light, signaled their success. The mist began to clear, revealing a new path leading out of the clearing.

Ethan looked around at his friends, his expression a mix of relief and determination. "We're making progress. But we can't let our guard down."

As they moved forward, the forest path led them to the next stage of their journey. Each step brought them closer to the next challenge, and the trials ahead would test them even further. With their spirits high and their resolve strengthened, they prepared for whatever lay ahead, knowing that each trial was a step closer to their ultimate goal.

Chapter 12: Labyrinth of Shadows

The forest path led the group to a cavern entrance, half-concealed by dense vines and overgrown foliage. The entrance was dark and foreboding, and a chill breeze emerged from within, carrying faint whispers of forgotten secrets. They paused at the threshold, each member feeling a mix of apprehension and determination.

"This is it," Ariana said, her voice steady despite the uncertainty in her eyes. "We need to enter and face whatever lies inside."

As they ventured into the cavern, the light from the forest behind them dimmed, and an unnatural darkness enveloped them. The walls of the cavern were lined with ancient symbols and runes that seemed to shift and change as they moved. The air was thick with an eerie silence, broken only by the sound of their footsteps echoing through the labyrinthine passages.

The cavern seemed to twist and turn endlessly, with corridors branching off in every direction. It was clear that this was no ordinary labyrinth; it was designed to test their resolve and cunning. Rahul took the lead, his divine weapon glowing faintly to illuminate their path.

"Stay close and keep your eyes open," Rahul instructed. "We can't afford to get lost in here."

As they navigated the winding passages, the walls began to close in, and the air grew colder. The labyrinth seemed to feed on their insecurities, manifesting doubts and fears.

Suddenly, the corridor ahead darkened, and a shadowy figure emerged. It was a spectral version of Rahul, dressed in the attire of a legendary prince. The specter's eyes glowed with an ominous light, and it wielded a sword that radiated dark energy.

The specter spoke in a voice that echoed Rahul's own. "You have the power of a prince, but do you have the strength to face your own darkness?"

Rahul's heart raced as he faced the apparition. The figure's presence was unnervingly familiar, a twisted reflection of his inner turmoil. He gripped his divine weapon tightly, ready to confront this challenge.

"This is just a trial," Rahul muttered to himself. "I can't let my fears control me."

The specter lunged with surprising speed. Rahul parried the attack, his divine weapon clashing against the specter's dark blade. The sound of metal against metal resonated through the cavern, and Rahul's focus narrowed to the fight at hand.

As the battle continued, Rahul began to see glimpses of his own fears reflected in the specter's attacks. The specter seemed to anticipate his moves, exploiting his doubts and hesitations. He struggled to maintain his composure, his mind racing with self-doubt.

"Why am I not strong enough?" he questioned silently. "Why can't I live up to my legacy?"

The specter's blade struck his side, and he staggered, feeling the weight of past failures pressing down on him. But he fought through the pain, focusing on the present battle rather than his past regrets.

With renewed determination, Rahul pressed on. Each strike was a challenge to his inner fears, each parry a testament to his strength. The specter's attacks grew more erratic as Rahul's resolve solidified.

Finally, with a powerful swing, Rahul defeated the specter. The shadowy figure dissipated into mist, leaving the cavern in a profound silence. Rahul stood panting, his heart pounding but his spirit unbroken.

The labyrinth's walls shifted, revealing a new path bathed in a soft, welcoming light. Rahul emerged from the trial, his sense of self and purpose strengthened. The group gathered, each member ready to face the next challenge, knowing that each trial brought them closer to their ultimate goal.

Chapter 13: Trial of the Guardian

As the group ventured further into the labyrinth, they came upon an eerie, vast chamber. At the center stood a massive stone pedestal, on which rested a glowing artifact—a shimmering shield etched with ancient symbols. The room was bathed in a ghostly light that seemed to pulse rhythmically, creating an almost hypnotic effect.

Nia stepped forward, her eyes drawn to the artifact. "This must be part of the trial," she said softly, sensing the protective energy emanating from the shield. "I can feel the power of the guardian spirit here."

As Nia approached the pedestal, the shadows around the chamber began to coalesce, forming into a formidable figure. The figure took shape as a spectral version of Nephthys, the Egyptian goddess of protection. Her eyes were cold and calculating, and her presence exuded a powerful aura of both strength and sorrow.

The specter spoke in a voice that resonated with both authority and melancholy. "To prove your worthiness, you must confront your deepest fears and showcase your true ability to protect. Only then will you be deemed worthy to claim the shield."

Nia's heart pounded in her chest. The specter's words struck a chord deep within her. She had always been the quiet, introverted student, and the weight of responsibility often felt like a burden. But now, in the face of this trial, she had to prove her worth.

"I am ready," Nia said, trying to steady her voice. She stepped closer to the pedestal, her hands reaching out to touch the shield. As she did, the chamber darkened, and shadows began to swirl around her, forming into nightmarish figures that embodied her greatest fears.

The first shadow took the form of a menacing creature, representing Nia's fear of inadequacy. It loomed over her, its eyes glowing with a cruel light. "You are not enough," it growled. "You cannot protect anyone."

Nia's breath hitched, but she steeled herself. "I am more than my fears," she said defiantly. "I have the strength to protect those I care about."

With a burst of energy, Nia summoned a protective barrier around herself, deflecting the creature's menacing attacks. The barrier shimmered with a bright light, reflecting her inner resolve and determination. The creature recoiled, its form dissipating into the shadows.

The next figure was a specter of a fallen ally, representing her fear of failure and loss. Its ghostly voice echoed in the chamber, mourning its defeat and accusing Nia of letting it down. "You failed me," it wailed. "You could have saved me."

Nia's heart ached, but she knew she had to confront this fear head-on. "I did everything I could," she said, her voice trembling but resolute. "I won't let my past failures dictate my future."

Drawing on her inner strength, Nia unleashed a wave of energy that banished the specter, her protective aura expanding to encompass the entire chamber. The shadows began to recede, and the light from the shield grew brighter, reflecting Nia's newfound confidence and ability to protect.

As the trial came to an end, the spectral Nephthys observed with a solemn nod. "You have proven yourself worthy," she intoned. "The shield is yours, a symbol of your true strength and dedication."

Nia approached the pedestal, her hands trembling slightly as she took the shield. The moment she touched it, she felt a surge of warmth and power, a confirmation of her worthiness. She held it close, feeling its protective energy resonate with her own spirit.

The labyrinth's walls shifted again, revealing a new passageway bathed in a soft, welcoming light. Nia joined the group, her heart uplifted by the trial's success. Each member of the group felt the weight of their individual trials, knowing that they were drawing closer to their ultimate goal.

The journey ahead was fraught with challenges, but with each trial, they grew stronger and more united, ready to face the darkness that threatened their world.

Chapter 14: Trial of the Tempest

The group continued their journey through the labyrinth, their path illuminated by the soft glow of Nia's new shield. They soon arrived at a vast, open cavern where the air crackled with electrical energy. The walls of the cavern were lined with ancient carvings depicting storms, lightning, and swirling tempests. At the center of the cavern, a large, cracked altar stood, pulsing with an eerie blue light.

Ethan's eyes widened as he approached the altar, feeling the familiar crackle of energy. "This is definitely a trial for me," he said, his voice filled with both excitement and apprehension. "I can feel the storm calling."

As Ethan approached the altar, the blue light intensified, and a storm seemed to materialize around them. Thunder rumbled, and lightning danced across the cavern walls, illuminating a shadowy figure that took shape in the center of the storm. The figure was a spectral representation of Thor, his eyes glowing with an electrifying intensity.

The specter's voice echoed with authority. "To prove your mastery over the tempest, you must face the storm within yourself. Only by controlling your own fury can you harness the true power of the storm."

Ethan clenched his fists, feeling a surge of frustration. He had always struggled with controlling his temper, and now he had to confront that very weakness. The specter's words seemed to cut deep, reflecting his inner turmoil.

The storm intensified, and lightning bolts began to strike the cavern floor, each one seeming to target Ethan. The raw power of the storm was overwhelming, and Ethan had to use all his strength to avoid the deadly bolts.

"Focus!" Ethan shouted to himself, his voice barely audible over the roaring storm. "I need to control this!"

He began to channel his energy, summoning his own lightning to counter the storm's attacks. His attempts were chaotic at first, with lightning bolts flashing erratically. He struggled to direct the energy, feeling his frustration rising with each failed attempt.

The storm seemed to respond to his anger, growing more violent and unpredictable. Ethan's control was slipping, and he felt as if he were being engulfed by the tempest. The specter of Thor watched with an inscrutable expression, offering no help or guidance.

As Ethan faced the storm's fury, he realized that his anger was making the situation worse. He had to find a way to calm himself and regain control. Taking a deep breath, he focused on channeling his energy with precision, using his frustration as fuel rather than letting it overwhelm him.

The storm's intensity began to wane as Ethan found his rhythm. He directed the lightning bolts with increasing accuracy, creating a dazzling display of controlled power. The specter of Thor nodded approvingly, and the storm began to abate.

With a final, powerful surge of energy, Ethan directed a bolt of lightning at the altar, causing it to crack open and reveal a glowing staff. The staff pulsed with the same blue light that had filled the cavern, a symbol of Ethan's mastery over the storm.

The storm clouds dissipated, and the cavern's lighting returned to normal. Ethan stood, panting and drenched, but triumphant. He approached the staff and took it in his hands, feeling its power resonate with his own.

The cavern walls shifted once more, revealing a new passage illuminated by a warm, inviting light. Ethan joined the group, his confidence renewed by the success of his trial. Each member of the team was growing stronger, and their unity was becoming more evident with every challenge they faced.

The journey ahead would test them further, but with each trial, they were one step closer to confronting the ancient evil that threatened their world.

Chapter 15: Trial of the Warrior

The group moved cautiously through the labyrinth, their spirits buoyed by their recent successes. They entered a new chamber, its walls lined with ancient battle scenes, depicting warriors engaged in epic clashes. In the center of the room stood a pedestal with a gleaming sword embedded in a stone block. The air was charged with the palpable tension of impending conflict.

Maya's eyes were drawn to the sword. "This must be the trial for me," she said, her voice tinged with determination. "It's time to see if I'm worthy of my role as a warrior."

As Maya approached the pedestal, the room darkened, and the walls began to glow with an eerie red light. The stone block shifted, and a new figure emerged from the shadows—a spectral embodiment of Mulan, her warrior armor glinting in the dim light.

The specter spoke with a commanding presence. "To prove your worth as a warrior, you must face the trials of combat and bravery. Only by overcoming these challenges will you earn the right to wield the sword."

Maya nodded, steeling herself for the challenge. As she reached for the sword, the ground beneath her feet began to tremble, and the chamber was suddenly filled with the sounds of clashing steel and battle cries. Shadowy warriors emerged from the darkness, their forms shifting and flickering like phantoms.

Maya drew on her training and skills, engaging the shadowy figures with swift, precise movements. Her martial arts training had prepared her for combat, but these spectral opponents were relentless and seemed to anticipate her every move.

The first shadowy warrior advanced, wielding a sword that seemed to blur with every swing. Maya parried its attacks with practiced skill, her movements fluid and graceful. But she soon realized that these opponents were not just physical threats; they also embodied her fears of failure and inadequacy.

"You're not strong enough!" one of the shadowy figures taunted. "You'll never be a true warrior!"

Maya's breath quickened, and she felt her confidence waver. She had always been driven by the fear of not measuring up, and these shadowy warriors seemed to exploit that weakness. She took a moment to center herself, recalling the strength and bravery of her past life as Mulan.

"No," Maya said firmly, her voice echoing with determination. "I am a warrior, and I will not let my fears control me."

Summoning her inner strength, Maya launched into a series of powerful strikes, her movements becoming a blur of precision and force. The shadowy warriors faltered under her relentless assault, their forms disintegrating with each blow.

The final trial came when the spectral Mulan appeared before Maya, her gaze piercing and stern. "You must face your ultimate fear: the possibility of failure. Only by overcoming this can you claim the sword."

The specter challenged Maya to a duel, and their clash was intense. The room reverberated with the sound of their battle, each strike and parry echoing with the weight of Maya's fears. But as the duel progressed, Maya began to find her rhythm, her movements becoming more fluid and confident.

With a final, decisive strike, Maya disarmed the spectral Mulan and stood victorious. The specter nodded in approval. "You have proven yourself worthy of the sword. It is now yours to wield."

Maya approached the pedestal and removed the sword from the stone block. The weapon felt perfectly balanced in her hands, a symbol of her strength and bravery. As she held it aloft, the chamber's lighting brightened, revealing a new passageway bathed in a warm, golden light.

The group regrouped, each member feeling the weight of their individual trials. Maya joined them, her confidence bolstered by her success. They continued on their journey, knowing that each challenge brought them closer to their ultimate goal.

The labyrinth was filled with more trials and dangers, but with each victory, they grew stronger and more unified. The path ahead was still uncertain, but their determination and resilience were unwavering.

Chapter 16: The Final Trial

The Eternal Guardians had made it through many trials, each one pushing their limits and revealing new facets of their powers. Yet, none were as daunting as the one that awaited them now. The chamber they entered was vast and eerie, lit only by flickering torches that cast long, wavering shadows across the walls. The air was thick with a sense of foreboding, and the temperature dropped noticeably as they stepped inside.

A stone pedestal stood in the center of the room, upon which rested an ancient, intricately carved box. The box was adorned with symbols and runes from various mythologies, their meanings long forgotten. The Guardians could feel the weight of the trial ahead, not just physically, but emotionally and mentally as well.

"Are we ready for this?" Maya asked, her voice tinged with a mix of anxiety and resolve.

"We've come this far," Rahul said, his tone steady. "We've faced challenges before. We can handle this."

Nia, her eyes scanning the room for any signs of danger, added, "We need to be cautious. This trial might be more than just a test of our powers."

A deep, resonant voice echoed through the chamber, emanating from the walls themselves. "Guardians, you have proven yourselves worthy to face the final trial. This trial is not one of individual prowess but of your ability to work as a cohesive unit. To succeed, you must face your deepest fears and insecurities—together."

As the voice faded, the stone box on the pedestal slowly creaked open. Inside, a swirling vortex of darkness and light began to form, growing larger and more intense. The room itself seemed to distort around them, warping and shifting in ways that defied logic.

The Guardians braced themselves as the vortex released a series of illusions, each tailored to exploit their greatest fears and vulnerabilities.

Ariana found herself in a dense, dark forest. The trees loomed tall and menacing, their branches clawing at her. She was alone, with no way to communicate with the others. The forest whispered with the voices of mythical creatures, taunting her. Her connection to nature felt severed, and she struggled to maintain her focus.

Rahul faced a vision of a grand battlefield, where he was surrounded by enemies and allies alike. The scene was chaotic, with familiar faces from his past appearing as foes. He was paralyzed by the weight of expectation, the burden of his legendary status making him doubt his abilities as a leader.

Nia was trapped in a dark void, with only a small circle of light surrounding her. Inside the circle were her friends, but they were unreachable, slowly fading away. Her protective instincts were useless in this void, and she felt helpless as the darkness closed in on her.

Ethan found himself in a stormy, desolate wasteland. Thunder roared, and lightning flashed violently, reflecting his own turbulent emotions. The storm seemed to be a physical manifestation of his inner turmoil, with his anger and frustration threatening to consume him.

Maya was in a grand hall filled with warriors from different eras, all of whom judged her harshly. Their gazes were cold and disapproving, questioning her worthiness as a warrior. Maya struggled to prove herself in a trial that seemed to challenge her very identity.

As each Guardian faced their personal trials, they were forced to confront their deepest fears and insecurities. The illusions were designed to break them apart, to make them question their unity and strength as a team.

But as the trials progressed, the Guardians began to realize that their fears were not insurmountable when faced together. They had learned to rely on each other's strengths, and this trial would be no different.

Ariana, finding herself in the heart of the forest, took a deep breath and tried to connect with her surroundings. She focused on her bond with nature, calling out to her friends in the hope that they could hear her. "We need to unite our strengths. We can't let our fears separate us."

Rahul, struggling with the weight of his responsibilities, heard Ariana's voice echoing through his battlefield. He realized that he couldn't face the challenges alone and needed to lead with the support of his team. "Ariana's right. We need to overcome this together."

Nia, trapped in her void, concentrated on the faint voices of her friends. She tried to use her protective instincts to shield herself and them from the encroaching darkness. "Stay with me. We're stronger together. I can feel your presence."

Ethan, battling the storm, heard the voices of his friends reaching him through the storm's chaos. He understood that his anger and frustration were obstacles that he could overcome with the help of his team. "I won't let this storm break me. We have to fight this together."

Maya, facing the disapproval of the warriors, realized that her worthiness as a warrior was not defined by others but by her own actions and beliefs. "I've fought for what's right. My friends believe in me, and that's what matters."

As each Guardian faced their fears, they began to see the illusions for what they were—mere obstacles designed to test their resolve. By reaching out to each other, they could see their fears dissipating, replaced by a shared strength and determination.

The chamber's atmosphere shifted as the Guardians' unity became palpable. The swirling vortex of darkness and light began to stabilize, its intensity fading as their combined efforts neutralized the illusions. The pedestal and the box slowly retreated, the trial coming to a close.

The room returned to its original state, the darkness lifting to reveal the exit. The Guardians stood together, their breaths heavy but their spirits high. They had faced their fears and emerged stronger, having proven that their unity was their greatest asset.

As they stepped through the exit, they knew that the final trial had been the ultimate test of their bond as a team. They were now ready to face whatever lay ahead, knowing that their strength was in their unity and their shared purpose as the Eternal Guardians.

Chapter 17: Reunion with the Gods

The Eternal Guardians stepped through the final trial's exit, feeling both triumphant and exhausted. The room they entered was bathed in a soft, celestial light, and the air was filled with a serene hum. They found themselves in a vast, open space with clouds floating beneath them like a fluffy carpet. The sky above was a deep, radiant blue, streaked with hues of gold and violet.

In the distance, two figures began to materialize, descending gracefully from the heavens. The first was a tall, athletic figure with an air of playful mischief about him. His winged sandals glinted as he landed softly on the cloud. The second figure was more imposing, with a regal bearing and a gaze that commanded respect. His aura exuded power and authority.

The Guardians recognized them immediately—Hermes and Zeus.

"Welcome, Guardians," Hermes greeted with a broad smile. "You've completed the trials. Not many can claim that honor."

Zeus nodded solemnly, his gaze sweeping over the group. "Indeed. Your journey has been arduous, but you have proven yourselves worthy. The final trial was a crucial test, not just of your individual strengths, but of your ability to work as one."

Ariana stepped forward, her eyes filled with both awe and determination. "We faced our fears and came through stronger. What's next for us?"

Hermes chuckled lightly. "You've done well, but there's still much to be done. The ancient evil you've been preparing for is growing stronger. It's not just a threat to the world but to the very fabric of our existence."

Rahul, always the leader, asked, "What can we do to stop it?"

Zeus's expression grew serious. "You have learned to harness your powers and work together. Now, you must prepare for the final battle. The evil forces are gathering, and they are formidable. You will need to be at your best, and you must rely on each other more than ever."

Nia, feeling the weight of their task, spoke up. "What exactly are we up against?"

Hermes's smile faded, replaced by a look of concern. "The ancient evil is known as Nyxar, a primordial being of darkness and chaos. It was sealed away long ago, but its influence is creeping back into the world. Nyxar seeks to unravel the balance between light and dark, and only you can stop it."

Maya's eyes narrowed with determination. "How do we find it? How do we defeat something that powerful?"

Zeus took a step forward, his voice carrying a tone of urgency. "Nyxar is hidden in a realm between worlds, accessible only through a series of ancient portals. You must find these portals and close them before Nyxar's return is complete. The trials you've faced have prepared you, but you will need to use all your skills and work together as never before."

Hermes nodded in agreement. "Each portal will test you in different ways. You will face more challenges, but remember that you are stronger together. Your bond as a team is your greatest weapon."

The Guardians exchanged determined looks. They had faced numerous trials, but the task ahead was their most daunting yet. They knew that their unity was their greatest strength and that they needed to trust each other completely.

Ariana took a deep breath and addressed her team. "We've come this far together. We can't stop now. Let's find these portals and stop Nyxar."

Rahul placed a reassuring hand on Ariana's shoulder. "We've faced our fears and overcome them. We'll face this next challenge as a team."

Nia nodded, her resolve firm. "We'll protect each other and fight for what's right."

Ethan, with a determined look, added, "We'll show Nyxar what we're made of."

Maya, her voice steady, concluded, "We'll face whatever comes our way. Together."

Zeus and Hermes exchanged satisfied glances. "We believe in you," Zeus said. "You are the chosen ones, and you have the power to protect the world from the darkness that threatens it."

Hermes extended his hand. "Good luck, Guardians. May your courage and unity guide you."

With a final nod from the gods, the Eternal Guardians felt a surge of energy and purpose. The sky shimmered, and the clouds parted to reveal a path leading to their next destination—a realm of uncertainty and challenge.

As they stepped forward, they knew that the journey ahead would test their strength, courage, and unity like never before. But with the guidance of the gods and their unwavering bond, they were ready to face whatever lay ahead and stop Nyxar from plunging the world into chaos.

Chapter 18: The Prophecy Unveiled

A s the celestial light dimmed and the vast expanse of clouds beneath them seemed to settle into a tranquil stillness, the Eternal Guardians gathered in a semi-circle around Zeus and Hermes. The weight of the task ahead hung heavily in the air, and the seriousness of their mission was reflected in their expressions.

Zeus raised his hand, calling for attention. His eyes, filled with an ancient wisdom, locked onto each of the Guardians in turn. "Before you embark on the next phase of your journey," he said, his voice echoing with the power of the heavens, "I must reveal to you a prophecy. It holds the key to finding the portals and stopping Nyxar."

The Guardians leaned in, eager to hear what the king of the gods had to say. The sky above them seemed to shimmer with anticipation, and the air around them grew charged with a palpable sense of destiny.

Zeus began, "In the days of old, when the world was young and the gods walked among men, there was a prophecy foretelling the rise of darkness and the coming of heroes to combat it. The prophecy speaks of five trials that will lead to the heart of the darkness, and each trial is linked to a hidden portal."

Hermes stepped forward, adding, "These portals are not easily found. They are concealed in realms that test your courage and unity. The prophecy will guide you, but you must decipher it with wisdom and bravery."

Zeus continued, "The prophecy reads as follows:"

"When the stars align and the moon hides her face,
Seek the paths where shadows trace.
Beneath the earth and beyond the sea,
The portals await where none can see.
The first lies where the waters roar,
The second in a land of lore.
The third in the midst of fire's blaze,
The fourth where ancient spirits gaze.
The last awaits where darkness reigns,
A place of trials and hidden chains.
Find these places, brave and true,
And close the doors where evil grew."

"This prophecy will lead you to the locations of the portals," Zeus explained. "But it is not merely a guide. It is a test of your resolve and your ability to interpret the signs."

Ariana furrowed her brow, absorbing the prophecy's cryptic message. "So, we have to find these places mentioned in the prophecy?"

Zeus nodded. "Exactly. Each location is hidden and protected by ancient magic. You will need to rely on your unique skills and work together to uncover them."

Rahul, always the strategist, asked, "How will we know when we're on the right track?"

Hermes smiled, his eyes twinkling with mischief. "The signs will reveal themselves as you approach each location. Trust in your instincts and your bond as a team. The trials will challenge you in ways you cannot foresee, but they will also reveal the strength within each of you."

Nia looked thoughtful. "What about the last trial? What does it mean by 'a place of trials and hidden chains'?"

Zeus's expression grew serious. "The last trial will be the most daunting. It will be a place of darkness and despair, where your greatest fears and weaknesses will be tested. But it is also where you will find the ultimate source of power to defeat Nyxar."

Maya's face hardened with resolve. "We've faced trials before. We'll face this one too."

Ethan, who had been listening intently, added, "So, we need to prepare ourselves not just physically but mentally. We'll need to be ready for anything."

Zeus nodded approvingly. "Yes. Prepare yourselves for the journey ahead. You will face dangers and challenges that will test every aspect of your being. But remember, you are not alone. The gods will guide you, and your unity will be your greatest strength."

Hermes stepped closer, placing a hand on each Guardian's shoulder. "You have already proven yourselves as heroes. Now, you must rise to the challenge and fulfill the prophecy. The fate of the world depends on you."

With these words, the sky above them began to shift, the clouds forming a gentle swirl as if beckoning them onward. The Guardians felt a renewed sense of purpose and determination. They knew that the journey ahead would be fraught with danger, but they were ready to face it.

As they prepared to leave, Zeus and Hermes offered their final words of encouragement. "Go forth with courage and wisdom," Zeus said. "The prophecy has set you on your path. Fulfill your destiny."

Hermes nodded, his expression both playful and serious. "And remember, even in the darkest moments, light can be found. Trust in yourselves and each other."

With a final glance at the gods, the Eternal Guardians set out on their quest, ready to face the trials ahead and decipher the prophecy that would lead them to the portals and ultimately to Nyxar. The adventure was far from over, but they were united and resolute, prepared to confront whatever lay ahead.

Chapter 19: The Roaring Waters

The Guardians found themselves standing on a rocky cliff, overlooking a vast ocean. The sound of crashing waves echoed in their ears, and the salty breeze whipped through their hair. The first line of the prophecy had led them here: "The first lies where the waters roar."

Ethan took a deep breath, the scent of the sea filling his lungs. "This must be the place. The roaring waters."

Ariana nodded, her keen senses alert to any signs of danger. "But where do we start? The ocean is vast."

Nia closed her eyes, focusing on the protective energy within her. "We should look for something out of the ordinary. The portal won't be in plain sight."

Rahul pointed to a narrow path winding down the cliffside. "There's a path leading down. Maybe it'll take us to what we're looking for."

Maya tightened the straps of her backpack. "Let's go, but stay alert. We don't know what kind of trial awaits us."

They descended the cliffside path, carefully navigating the uneven terrain. As they reached the shoreline, the waves grew louder and more intense. The ocean seemed almost alive, its power a constant reminder of the trial ahead.

Ethan's eyes scanned the horizon. "There!" He pointed to a small island barely visible through the mist. "That's where we need to go."

Ariana furrowed her brow. "How do you know?"

Ethan shrugged. "Call it a hunch. Or maybe Thor's instincts."

Rahul nodded. "We trust your instincts, Ethan. Let's find a way to get there."

As they searched for a boat or raft, they noticed a set of ancient, weathered stones protruding from the water, forming a rough pathway towards the island. It was barely visible amidst the waves, but it was their only option.

"Looks like we'll be walking," Maya said, eyeing the stones warily.

One by one, they stepped onto the slippery stones, the water surging around them with every step. It was a precarious journey, requiring balance and focus. The waves seemed to grow more aggressive, as if testing their resolve.

Nia was the first to slip, her foot sliding off a stone and plunging into the cold water. She gasped, but Ethan grabbed her arm, steadying her.

"Got you," he said, pulling her back onto the path.

"Thanks," Nia replied, regaining her balance.

They continued, each step a challenge against the roaring waters. When they finally reached the island, they were soaked and shivering, but their determination remained unshaken.

The island was small and rocky, with a dense thicket of trees at its center. The air was thick with the scent of salt and earth, and the sound of the waves crashing against the rocks was deafening.

Ariana led the way into the thicket, her senses attuned to the natural world around her. "There's something here," she said, pushing aside the branches.

In the center of the thicket, they found a small clearing. At its heart stood an ancient stone altar, covered in intricate carvings of sea creatures and stormy waves.

"This must be it," Rahul said, examining the altar. "But what do we do?"

Ethan stepped forward, feeling a strange pull towards the altar. He placed his hands on the stone, and a surge of power coursed through him. The carvings began to glow with a soft, blue light.

A deep voice echoed in their minds, resonating with the power of the ocean. "To pass this trial, you must confront the fury of the sea and the strength within."

Suddenly, the ground beneath them trembled, and a column of water erupted from the altar, forming a towering figure made entirely of water. It loomed over them, its eyes glowing with a fierce, otherworldly light.

Ethan stepped forward, summoning his courage. "I'll handle this. It's my trial."

The water figure roared, and the waves around the island grew more violent. Ethan summoned the power of Thor, electricity crackling around him. He met the water figure's gaze, his eyes filled with determination.

"You think you can scare me?" Ethan shouted. "I am Thor, god of thunder!"

The water figure lunged at him, but Ethan stood his ground. He raised his hands, calling upon the storm. Thunder rumbled in the sky, and lightning struck the water figure, sending a shower of steam and sparks into the air.

But the figure reformed, more powerful than before. Ethan realized he couldn't rely on brute strength alone. He needed to understand the true nature of his opponent.

Closing his eyes, Ethan focused on the rhythm of the waves and the power of the sea. He felt the connection between himself and the water figure, realizing it was a manifestation of the ocean's fury and strength.

"I understand now," he whispered. "I need to embrace the power within, not fight against it."

Opening his eyes, Ethan lowered his hands and took a deep breath. The water figure paused, sensing the change in him. Ethan extended his hand towards the figure, and the electricity around him dissipated.

The figure's eyes softened, and it lowered its form, becoming calm and still. Ethan stepped forward, placing his hand on the figure's chest. The water figure dissolved into a gentle stream, flowing back into the altar.

The blue light from the carvings intensified, and a portal opened at the base of the altar. Ethan turned to his friends, a smile of triumph on his face.

"We did it," he said. "The first portal is open."

Rahul clapped him on the back. "Great job, Ethan. You showed true strength and wisdom."

Nia nodded. "And you controlled your temper. That's growth."

Maya smiled. "One trial down, five to go."

Ariana looked at the portal, her eyes filled with determination. "Let's keep moving. We've got a world to save."

With renewed resolve, the Guardians stepped through the portal, ready to face the next trial and unlock the secrets of the prophecy. The journey was far from over, but they were stronger together, and their bond would carry them through the challenges ahead.

Chapter 20: The Land of Lore

The Guardians emerged from the portal into a realm that seemed to straddle the line between reality and legend. Towering trees with golden leaves, glowing flora, and mythical creatures roamed freely. The air was thick with enchantment, and a sense of ancient magic permeated the landscape.

Ariana took in the surroundings, her eyes wide with wonder. "This place is... incredible. It's like we've stepped into a myth."

Nia nodded, her protective instincts heightened. "We need to stay focused. The prophecy mentioned this place as a land of lore. We should expect the unexpected."

Rahul pointed towards a path lined with ancient stone markers, each inscribed with runes. "That path looks like it leads to something important. Let's follow it."

As they walked along the path, they noticed the runes glowing faintly. Ethan touched one, feeling a slight vibration. "These stones are charged with magic. We're definitely on the right track."

The path led them to a grand clearing where a massive, ancient tree stood. Its roots twisted and intertwined, creating a natural archway. At the base of the tree, a wise old sage sat cross-legged, meditating. He wore robes that shimmered like the night sky, and his long beard flowed like a river of stars.

The sage opened his eyes as the Guardians approached. "Welcome, Eternal Guardians. I have been expecting you."

Rahul stepped forward, his voice respectful. "We are here to find the second portal. The prophecy led us to this land of lore."

The sage nodded. "Indeed. To unlock the portal, each of you must face a challenge that will test your understanding of your own strengths and weaknesses. Only by embracing your true selves can you proceed."

He waved his hand, and the ground beneath them shimmered. The Guardians found themselves standing in individual circles of light, each separated from the others. The sage's voice echoed in their minds. "Focus on your inner self, and the challenge will reveal itself."

Ariana found herself in a dense forest, surrounded by animals. The creatures looked to her for guidance, their eyes filled with trust. She realized her challenge was to embrace her role as a protector. Drawing on her bond with nature, she led the animals to safety, feeling a deep connection with each step.

Rahul stood in a battlefield, shadowy figures charging towards him. He had to rely on his leadership and combat skills to protect those around him. Using his strategic mind and warrior instincts, he defended his allies, his actions driven by the responsibility of his legendary identity.

Nia was in a labyrinth, the walls shifting and changing. Her challenge was to navigate the maze using her protective powers and intuition. She created barriers of light to guide her path, trusting in her inner strength to lead her through the twists and turns.

Ethan found himself on a stormy mountaintop, thunder and lightning crashing around him. His challenge was to control the storm within. By calming his mind and embracing the power of Thor, he balanced the tempest, finding harmony in the chaos.

Maya stood in an ancient temple, surrounded by warrior spirits. She had to prove her worth as a fighter and a leader. Drawing on her martial arts skills and the courage of Mulan, she faced each spirit with honor, her movements precise and powerful.

One by one, the Guardians overcame their challenges, their circles of light merging into a single, radiant beam. They found themselves back in the clearing, the sage smiling warmly.

"You have each demonstrated the qualities that make you true Guardians," he said. "The second portal is now open."

The ancient tree's roots parted, revealing a glowing portal beneath. The Guardians gathered around, their bond stronger than ever.

"Ready for the next trial?" Ethan asked, a confident grin on his face.

Rahul nodded. "We've got this. Let's go."

With a deep breath, they stepped through the portal, emerging into a new realm filled with volcanic landscapes and rivers of molten lava. The heat was intense, and the air was thick with ash and smoke.

A deep voice rumbled from the fiery depths. "Welcome to the Valley of Flames. To proceed, you must withstand the heat of the fire and the trials of the flame."

Maya looked around, her eyes steely with determination. "We've faced water and lore. Now, we face fire. Let's find the third portal and show this realm what we're made of."

Together, the Guardians ventured into the scorching landscape, ready to confront the next trial and continue their quest to fulfill the prophecy and save the world.

Chapter 21: The Flames of Trial

The Guardians trekked through the volcanic landscape, the ground beneath their feet hot and unstable. Rivers of molten lava flowed around them, and the air shimmered with heat. Despite the oppressive environment, their resolve remained unbroken.

Ethan wiped the sweat from his brow. "This place is brutal. We need to stay focused and find the next trial."

Rahul scanned the horizon. "The prophecy mentioned fire's blaze. There must be something here that will lead us to the portal."

Ariana pointed to a towering volcano in the distance, its peak glowing with fiery light. "That volcano seems like a good place to start."

Nia nodded, her protective aura shimmering around her. "Let's move quickly. This heat is draining our energy."

As they approached the base of the volcano, the ground rumbled, and a figure emerged from the molten rock. It was a fire elemental, its body composed entirely of flames and lava. Its eyes glowed with an intense, fiery light.

"You have entered the Valley of Flames," the elemental boomed. "To proceed, you must prove your resilience and strength. Only one of you may face this trial."

Maya stepped forward, her determination evident. "This is my trial. I will face the flames."

The elemental nodded, its fiery form crackling. "Very well. Step into the circle and let the trial begin."

A ring of fire formed around Maya, the heat intensifying. She took a deep breath, her mind focused on the task ahead. The flames roared, but she stood her ground, drawing on her inner strength and the courage of Mulan.

The elemental raised its arms, and pillars of fire erupted around Maya. She dodged and weaved, her movements swift and precise. Each step was a dance of survival, her martial arts training guiding her through the fiery onslaught.

"Remember your training, Maya," she whispered to herself. "Stay calm, stay focused."

The flames grew hotter, and the elemental's attacks more relentless. Maya's skin burned, but she pushed through the pain, her determination unwavering. She summoned the spirit of Mulan, her willpower and resilience shining through.

Finally, the elemental paused, its fiery form flickering. "You have proven your strength and resilience, warrior. The portal is now open."

The ring of fire dissipated, revealing a portal at the base of the volcano. Maya turned to her friends, a triumphant smile on her face.

"We did it," she said, her voice filled with relief. "The third portal is open."

Rahul clapped her on the back. "You were amazing, Maya. Your strength and courage are an inspiration."

Nia nodded, her protective aura shimmering. "You've shown us what it means to face the flames and emerge stronger."

Ethan grinned. "We're halfway there. Let's keep this momentum going."

They gathered around the portal, their bond strengthened by the trials they had faced. With a deep breath, they stepped through, emerging into a realm of ancient spirits and forgotten memories.

The air was cool and filled with the whispers of long-lost souls. Ethereal lights floated around them, casting an eerie glow. The ground was covered in moss and fallen leaves, the remnants of an ancient forest.

"This place feels... different," Ariana said, her voice hushed. "Like it's filled with history and memories."

Rahul nodded. "The prophecy mentioned ancient spirits. We must be in the realm where they gaze."

Nia looked around, her protective instincts heightened. "We need to be cautious. This place is filled with unseen dangers."

As they ventured deeper into the realm, they encountered spectral figures, their eyes filled with sorrow and longing. The Guardians knew that their next trial would test their understanding of the past and their ability to connect with the spirits.

A voice echoed through the realm, soft and mournful. "To proceed, you must face the memories of the past and find the truth within."

Ethan stepped forward, his expression serious. "We're ready. Show us the way."

The spectral figures parted, revealing a path lined with ancient trees. The Guardians knew that their journey was far from over, but they were ready to face whatever trials awaited them in this land of memories and spirits.

With determination in their hearts and unity in their steps, they walked forward, ready to uncover the secrets of the past and continue their quest to fulfill the prophecy and save the world.

Chapter 22: The Spirits' Gaze

The Guardians moved cautiously along the path, the whispers of ancient spirits echoing around them. The air was thick with memories, each step feeling like a journey through time. The spectral figures watched them silently, their eyes filled with an otherworldly wisdom.

Ariana felt a shiver run down her spine. "This place is filled with so much history. I can almost hear their stories."

Nia nodded. "We need to be respectful. These spirits have witnessed countless ages and hold knowledge we can't even fathom."

As they approached a clearing, a large, ancient tree stood at its center. Its branches stretched high into the sky, covered in glowing, ethereal leaves. The ground around the tree was dotted with small, glowing stones, each one pulsing with a gentle light.

A soft voice emanated from the tree, resonating with the power of ages past. "To proceed, you must face the memories of the past and find the truth within."

Rahul stepped forward, his expression resolute. "This is my trial. I will face the memories and uncover the truth."

The tree's voice continued. "Touch the stones and let the memories flow. Only by understanding the past can you secure the future."

Rahul approached the stones, his heart pounding. He knelt down and placed his hand on one of the glowing stones. Instantly, his mind was flooded with visions of ancient battles, heroic deeds, and sacrifices made in the name of justice.

He saw glimpses of his past life as Rama, fighting against the forces of darkness, leading armies, and making difficult decisions for the greater good. The memories were overwhelming, but Rahul focused on the lessons they held.

"Remember who you are," he whispered to himself. "Learn from the past, but do not be consumed by it."

The visions shifted, showing moments of doubt and fear, times when even Rama questioned his path. Rahul felt a deep connection to these memories, understanding the weight of leadership and the loneliness that often accompanied it.

The tree's voice spoke again, gentle and encouraging. "You are not alone, Rahul. You have your friends, your allies. Trust in them and in yourself."

As the final vision faded, Rahul opened his eyes, feeling a renewed sense of clarity and purpose. He stood up, turning to face the Guardians, a look of determination on his face.

"I've seen the past," he said. "And I understand what I must do. We need to learn from our experiences, support each other, and face the challenges together."

The tree's branches rustled, and a portal appeared at its base, glowing with a soft, ethereal light. "You have passed the trial. The portal is now open."

The Guardians gathered around the portal, their spirits lifted by Rahul's courage and insight. They prepared to step through, but the scene around them seemed to shift, expanding in their vision.

They looked around and saw the world of shadows and darkness surrounding them, vast and desolate. The ground was barren and cracked, stretching out into the distance, with twisted, gnarled trees and shifting shadows creating a maze of uncertainty. The sky above was perpetually twilight, casting an eerie glow over the landscape.

A cold wind swept through, carrying with it the whispers of long-forgotten voices. The air was thick with an unsettling silence, broken only by the distant echoes of unseen creatures. The landscape seemed to pulse with a dark energy, hinting at the dangers that lay hidden within its depths.

The Guardians knew that this world was the final stage of their journey, a place where their unity and strength would be tested like never before. They could sense the weight of the trials yet to come, but they also felt a deep resolve within themselves. They had faced countless challenges and emerged stronger each time.

As they took in the desolate beauty of the world around them, they felt a sense of both awe and trepidation. The darkness here was profound, but it was a darkness they had come to understand. They knew that their bond and their courage would light the way forward.

With a final glance at each other, they prepared to face the next trial, ready to confront whatever shadows lay ahead. They were united in their purpose, their hearts and minds focused on the prophecy and the fate of the world. The journey was far from over, but they were ready to embrace the challenges that awaited them, confident in their strength and the power of their friendship.

Chapter 23: Clash of Shadows

The Guardians stepped through the portal, finding themselves in a new and foreboding world. The air was heavy with darkness, and the landscape stretched out in a twisted, eerie expanse. The sky was a swirling mass of dark clouds, occasionally illuminated by flashes of ominous lightning. The ground was uneven and cracked, with strange, shadowy formations jutting up like twisted fingers.

As they cautiously advanced, the Guardians could sense that they were not alone. An unsettling silence pervaded the area, broken only by the distant echoes of what seemed like whispers in the dark. They remained vigilant, each step taken with a sense of growing unease.

Suddenly, the silence was shattered by the sound of a distant, guttural roar. From the shadows, figures began to emerge, their forms shifting and flickering like dark flames. The creatures were unlike anything the Guardians had faced before.

The minions of Nyxar had arrived.

The first group of minions emerged from the darkness with a chilling presence. They were tall, sinewy creatures with elongated limbs and glowing red eyes that pierced through the shadows. Their skin was a mottled gray, with dark, jagged lines running across their bodies, giving them a grotesque, almost skeletal appearance. Their movements were swift and jerky, as if they were being controlled by an unseen force. Their claws and fangs were sharp, and they emitted a low, eerie growl that sent shivers down the spines of the Guardians.

A second wave of minions followed, more formidable and imposing. These were larger, armored beings with dark, metallic plating covering their bodies. Their eyes glowed an eerie green, and they wielded wickedly sharp weapons, including massive swords and spiked maces. Their armor was adorned with ancient, sinister runes that seemed to pulse with dark energy. They moved with a calculated, menacing grace, their every step resonating with a heavy, echoing thud.

Lastly, the most terrifying of all emerged—the shadow wraiths. These ethereal beings were almost intangible, their forms constantly shifting and writhing like dark smoke. They had no distinct features, only dark, swirling masses that seemed to absorb light. Their presence was accompanied by a cold, oppressive aura that made the air feel suffocating. They could pass through solid objects and strike with an unseen force, making them especially dangerous.

As the minions closed in, the Guardians readied themselves for battle. Ethan, his eyes glowing with the power of Thor, stepped forward. "We've got to hold them off! We can't let them overwhelm us."

Rahul nodded, his expression resolute. "Stay together and watch each other's backs. We can't afford to be separated."

Nia extended her hands, calling upon her protective powers. A shimmering barrier formed around the group, deflecting the initial onslaught of the minions. "I'll keep us shielded, but I need you all to fight with everything you've got."

The tall, sinewy creatures lunged forward, their claws slashing through the air. Maya met them head-on, her martial arts training coming into play. She dodged and countered with precise strikes, her movements fluid and graceful. Each kick and punch landed with a resounding impact, sending several of the creatures reeling.

The armored minions charged with their weapons drawn. Rahul met their advance with his own blade, his strength and skill evident as he parried their strikes and counterattacked with powerful blows. He moved with the confidence of a seasoned warrior, each swing of his sword cutting through the dark armor of his foes.

Ethan faced the shadow wraiths, his lightning crackling through the air. The wraiths seemed to dissipate and reform with each strike, their intangible forms making them difficult to hit. Ethan focused his power, channeling it into concentrated bolts of lightning that illuminated the darkness with blinding flashes.

Ariana, meanwhile, used her connection to nature to summon ethereal creatures from the surrounding environment. Ghostly animals—wolves, hawks, and deer—emerged from the shadows, joining the battle. They attacked the minions with fierce determination, their presence adding to the chaotic melee.

The battle raged on, each Guardian pushing their abilities to the limit. Nia's barrier held firm, but the strain of maintaining it was evident. She could feel the dark energy of the minions pressing against her shield, testing her resolve.

As the fight continued, the Guardians began to notice that the minions' numbers were seemingly endless. Each fallen enemy seemed to be replaced by another, emerging from the shadows with relentless determination. It became clear that the minions were not just fighting to defeat them but to wear them down, to exhaust their strength and resolve.

Amidst the chaos, Rahul caught sight of a figure in the distance—a tall, imposing silhouette shrouded in darkness. It was Nyxar himself, watching from the shadows, his eyes glowing with a sinister light. He was not participating in the battle but rather observing, as if waiting for the right moment to strike.

The Guardians fought valiantly, their efforts united in their struggle against the seemingly insurmountable odds. The echoes of battle mixed with the roars of the minions and the clashing of weapons, creating a cacophony of sound that filled the darkened world.

Despite the overwhelming odds, the Guardians remained steadfast. Their bond and determination fueled their fight, each of them pushing through the exhaustion and pain. They knew that the outcome of this battle would determine their fate and the fate of the world they were fighting to protect.

Chapter 24: The Dark Trap

The clash between the Guardians and Nyxar's minions was fierce, but as the last of the shadowy creatures fell, the battlefield fell silent. Exhausted and battered, the Guardians took a moment to catch their breath. The dense darkness that surrounded them seemed to grow heavier, an oppressive weight that matched their fatigue.

Just as they began to regroup, a chilling breeze swept through the area, and a new figure emerged from the shadows. Nyxar himself stepped into view, his presence commanding and menacing. His form was imposing, shrouded in darkness with eyes glowing like molten gold. His aura radiated an intense, oppressive energy that seemed to warp the very fabric of reality around him.

The Guardians turned to face him, their weapons drawn and their stances ready. Ethan, his chest heaving from the exertion, took a step forward. "So, you're the one behind all of this."

Nyxar's voice was deep and resonant, carrying an almost musical quality to it despite its malevolence. "Indeed. I see you've fought bravely, but it seems you've been led to believe that you were merely facing trials."

Rahul tightened his grip on his sword, his eyes narrowing. "What are you talking about?"

Nyxar smiled, a cold, calculating expression that sent shivers down their spines. "The trials you've faced were not supposed to be so simple. I had intended to make them far more difficult, but I chose to make them easier for you. I wanted to see how you would handle my ultimate trap."

Maya's face twisted with anger. "You're saying this was all a setup? That you were playing with us?"

Nyxar's gaze swept over them, his expression one of cold amusement. "Precisely. You have walked right into my trap. And now, you will pay the price."

Without another word, Nyxar raised his hands, and the ground beneath them began to tremble. Dark tendrils of energy erupted from the earth, wrapping around the Guardians' legs and pulling them down. The darkness seemed to seep into their very beings, sapping their strength and willpower.

Nia struggled against the dark energy, her barrier flickering as it fought to hold back the encroaching shadows. "We need to fight it! We can't let him win!"

Ariana called upon her connection to nature, summoning ethereal creatures to help fend off the darkness. But the more they fought, the stronger the shadows seemed to become. Nyxar's dark magic was overwhelming, and the Guardians found themselves struggling to maintain their footing.

Ethan summoned his lightning, hoping to drive back the dark tendrils. Bolts of electricity crackled through the air, but they had little effect. The shadows absorbed the energy, growing even more potent in response.

Nyxar laughed, a deep, resonant sound that echoed through the darkness. "Your efforts are futile. My power is far beyond anything you can comprehend. You are merely pawns in my game."

Rahul's blade struck out at the shadows, but each swing seemed to vanish into the darkness, achieving nothing. His breathing was ragged, his strength waning with each failed attempt. "We can't keep this up! We need a plan!"

But Nyxar was relentless. He advanced towards them, his dark energy intensifying. "Your struggle is admirable, but it changes nothing. You are trapped in my domain, and there is no escape."

The Guardians fought with every ounce of their remaining strength, their determination unwavering even in the face of overwhelming odds. But Nyxar's power was insurmountable. He seemed to be everywhere at once, his presence an all-encompassing darkness that swallowed their attacks and diminished their hope.

As the battle dragged on, exhaustion began to take its toll. The Guardians' movements became sluggish, their breaths labored. The shadows tightened their grip, pulling them further into the darkness. Their earlier victories felt like distant memories, overshadowed by the crushing reality of their situation.

Despite their best efforts, Nyxar remained untouchable. His dark magic was too powerful, his control over the shadows too complete. Each time the Guardians thought they had gained an upper hand, Nyxar's dark energy would surge forth, reinforcing his trap and pushing them back.

The fight continued, but it was clear that Nyxar was unbeatable. The darkness around them seemed to pulse with a life of its own, responding to Nyxar's will and amplifying his power. The Guardians fought on, their resolve unbroken even as their strength waned, knowing that every battle had its cost and that this one was far from over.

Chapter 25: The Divine Intervention

As Nyxar's oppressive darkness tightened its grip around them, the Guardians felt their strength draining away. The shadows were relentless, and Nyxar's malevolent presence was suffocating. Despair threatened to overwhelm them, but amidst the chaos, a flicker of hope remained.

Nia, her voice straining against the darkness, shouted, "We need help! We can't do this alone. Gods, if you're listening, we need you now!"

Her words were almost swallowed by the roaring darkness, but the Guardians clung to the faint hope that their call had been heard. Ethan, barely able to lift his head, channeled what remained of his energy into a plea. "Please! Help us!"

Rahul, struggling to stay upright, joined in the desperate call. "We're fighting as hard as we can, but this darkness is too much!"

Ariana, sensing the urgency, closed her eyes and reached out with her connection to the natural world, hoping that the gods would respond to their call. "We've fought so hard. We need your strength now!"

As the darkness seemed to close in, a sudden and intense light began to pierce through the shadows. The energy was blinding, a pure, radiant force that cut through Nyxar's oppressive presence. The Guardians shielded their eyes, feeling the warmth and power of the divine light enveloping them.

In an instant, the battlefield around them dissolved into shimmering light. The crushing darkness gave way to a vast, ethereal space. The

Guardians found themselves standing in a magnificent palace, its grandeur beyond anything they had ever imagined. The palace was an otherworldly blend of celestial elegance and divine power, with towering columns of crystal and walls adorned with symbols from countless mythologies.

The Guardians looked around in awe, their breaths catching at the sight. They stood before a council of gods from various pantheons—Greek, Egyptian, Norse, and others. Each deity was surrounded by an aura of immense power, their presence both commanding and reassuring.

Zeus, his eyes filled with the weight of the situation, addressed the Guardians with a solemn tone. "You have called upon us in your darkest hour. We will not fight your battle for you, but we will guide you."

Odin, his one eye gleaming with ancient wisdom, nodded. "Nyxar has joined forces with many evil entities, and his dark influence extends far beyond what you have faced. We must devise a plan to counter this threat."

Ra, his golden radiance illuminating the room, spoke with authority. "We must understand the full scope of Nyxar's alliances and the strengths of his forces. Only then can we hope to turn the tide of this conflict."

The Guardians gathered around the divine council, their exhaustion momentarily forgotten in the face of this extraordinary opportunity. They discussed the situation, the gods providing insights into the enemy's strengths and weaknesses.

Zeus explained, "Nyxar's alliance includes ancient evils and dark forces from many realms. His army is vast and powerful, bolstered by creatures and dark sorcery."

Odin added, "To defeat him, you must strike at the heart of his power. He has used your trials as a means to trap you and to weaken your resolve."

Ra's voice was firm. "Our combined power can aid you, but you must be prepared for the final confrontation. The path ahead will be fraught with challenges, and you must use the knowledge and strength you have gained to face them."

The gods' counsel was invaluable, providing the Guardians with a clearer understanding of their enemy and the path forward. The Guardians were filled with a renewed sense of purpose, their earlier despair replaced by a strategic resolve.

Zeus raised his hand, and a celestial map appeared, showing the locations of Nyxar's strongholds and the key points of their battle plan. "Study this map. It will guide you in your next steps. The battles to come will be arduous, but you have the strength and wisdom to overcome them."

With their plan in place and their spirits lifted by the divine guidance, the Guardians prepared to return to the battlefield. The gods' presence had given them the clarity and strength they needed to confront Nyxar and his dark forces.

The radiant palace began to dissolve, the light enveloping the Guardians once more. As they were transported back to their world, they were ready to face the next trial with the knowledge and support they had gained from the gods. The battle was far from over, but they were now equipped with the divine insight and strategy needed to fight back against the encroaching darkness.

Chapter 26: The Celestial Assembly

As the Guardians took in their surroundings, their exhaustion momentarily forgotten, they found themselves in the presence of a divine council. Gods from various pantheons—Greek, Egyptian, Norse, and others—stood around a grand, circular table that seemed to float in midair. Their forms were both awe-inspiring and comforting, their power resonating through the very air.

Zeus, resplendent in his regal attire, his eyes shimmering with ancient wisdom, was the first to address them. "Welcome, Guardians. You have summoned us in your hour of need. We shall not fight your battle for you, but we will guide you with our knowledge and power."

Odin, his one eye gleaming with deep knowledge, nodded in agreement. "Nyxar's forces are vast and formidable, consisting of ancient evils and dark entities from many realms. To counter this threat, we must devise a strategy that addresses both his military strength and the dark magic that empowers him."

Ra, glowing with a golden radiance, spoke with authority. "Our combined strength is unparalleled, but to defeat Nyxar, you must act strategically. We will provide you with insights and support, but you must be prepared to execute a detailed plan."

The Guardians gathered around the celestial table, their weariness replaced by renewed focus. A luminous map appeared above the table, displaying Nyxar's strongholds and key points of interest. The map pulsed with a soft, otherworldly light, highlighting areas of strategic importance.

Zeus pointed to various locations on the map. "Nyxar's strongholds are spread across multiple realms. Each stronghold is fortified with dark magic and powerful minions. Our first objective is to disrupt his supply lines and weaken his forces. We have identified several key locations where you can launch effective strikes."

Odin leaned forward, his gaze sharp and calculating. "The dark sorcery that Nyxar commands is tied to these strongholds. If you can infiltrate these locations and neutralize them, you will diminish his magical power and reduce his overall strength. Prioritize these sites to cripple his ability to wage war."

Ra's voice was steady and commanding. "You will need more than just strategy. We can summon allies from various realms to aid you in your efforts. However, it is crucial to coordinate these forces carefully. Strike at multiple points simultaneously to stretch his defenses thin and create openings for decisive blows."

The Guardians absorbed the information, their determination growing stronger with each passing moment. The celestial map showed detailed routes and critical points, providing a clear path forward. The gods' counsel had given them a strategic advantage, but the path ahead was still fraught with challenges.

Zeus raised his hand, and a series of shimmering sigils appeared around the map, representing different divine and mortal forces that could be summoned. "These sigils represent our potential allies. We will call upon them to assist you, but it is up to you to lead and unify these forces against Nyxar."

Odin's voice carried a note of caution. "Remember, Nyxar's dark influence is pervasive. His allies are cunning and dangerous. You must be prepared for deception and betrayal. Trust your instincts and rely on the strength of your unity."

Ra offered a final piece of guidance. "Our combined power will aid you in the final confrontation. But you must be vigilant and adaptable. The battle ahead will test your resolve, but with the knowledge and support we have provided, you stand a strong chance of victory."

With their plan in place and their spirits lifted by the divine guidance, the Guardians felt a renewed sense of purpose. The celestial assembly had provided them with not just a strategy, but also the hope and determination needed to confront the darkness ahead.

As the radiant palace began to dissolve once more, enveloping them in a warm, celestial light, the Guardians readied themselves to return to their world. They were now equipped with the divine insight and strategy necessary to face Nyxar and his dark forces.

Back in the realm of shadows, the Guardians prepared for the imminent battles. The divine guidance had fortified their resolve, and they were ready to lead the charge against the encroaching darkness. With unity, strength, and strategic prowess, they set out to confront the looming threat, knowing that the fate of all realms rested on their shoulders.

The final confrontation was drawing near, and the Guardians were poised to meet it with all the strength and determination they could muster.

Chapter 27: The Gathering Storm

As the celestial plan took shape, the gods and their allies prepared for the monumental battle ahead. The Guardians stood alongside their divine allies, each figure radiating power and resolve. The battlefield was set to be a clash of epic proportions, with the fate of all realms hanging in the balance.

Zeus, with a commanding voice that resonated through the assembled forces, addressed the crowd. "We are on the brink of a great conflict. Nyxar's dark forces are numerous, but our unity and strength will turn the tide."

Odin, leaning on his staff, added, "We have analyzed the enemy's numbers. Their armies are vast, with countless dark creatures and sorcerers. But we have the advantage of our combined might and strategic insight."

Ra, glowing with golden light, spoke of their preparations. "Our forces are ready, and our strategy is sound. We will strike at the heart of Nyxar's strongholds, severing the connections he has with his dark allies."

The Guardians, despite their exhaustion, stood tall. They were ready to lead their respective factions into battle, bolstered by the support and guidance of the gods. Each leader briefed their troops, their voices filled with determination and hope.

Rahul gathered his followers, his voice unwavering. "We will break through their defenses and reach Nyxar. Our mission is clear: dismantle his power structure and confront him directly."

Ariana spoke to the woodland and animal allies, who were primed for the fight. "Nature itself will aid us in this battle. We will use every resource at our disposal to protect our world."

Ethan, rallying his companions, said, "We have the power and the will to overcome this darkness. Let's show them what we're made of."

Maya, with her martial prowess, prepared her warriors. "We'll strike with precision and strength. This is our moment to prove our valor."

The armies assembled, each contingent ready for the challenge ahead. The celestial map showed their coordinated movements, a detailed plan to strike at Nyxar's strongholds and weaken his forces.

As the troops prepared to march, a sense of impending doom loomed over the assembled ranks. The skies darkened as if in response to the approaching battle, and a foreboding chill crept through the air.

Zeus, with a grave expression, turned to the Guardians. "Remember, this battle is but the beginning. Nyxar's power is deeply rooted, and even with our combined forces, the true fight is yet to come."

Just as the armies were about to mobilize, a sudden and unexpected tremor shook the ground. The celestial map flickered, revealing an ominous new development.

Odin's eye widened in alarm. "Something's wrong. There's an anomaly in our calculations—an unknown force."

Ra's golden aura dimmed slightly as he observed the map. "This could be a trap or a new threat. We need to investigate immediately."

As the Guardians and the gods focused on the map, a dark figure emerged from the shadows. It was Nyxar, his presence unmistakable and terrifying. He stood alone, his eyes glowing with malevolent triumph.

With a chilling voice that echoed through the realm, Nyxar proclaimed, "You think you're prepared for battle? I've been waiting for you. But you're not the only ones with tricks up their sleeves."

In a blinding flash, the map disintegrated, and a new, nightmarish vision appeared. It was a colossal, swirling vortex of dark energy, swirling with the remnants of Nyxar's dark magic. The sight was horrifying, a stark representation of a powerful, hidden force that could turn the tide of the impending battle.

Nyxar's voice reverberated through the vision. "Behold the true weapon of my wrath. A force beyond your wildest fears, one that I've kept hidden until now. Prepare yourselves for what is to come, for this battle will test the very limits of your strength and unity."

As the vision faded and the darkness receded, the Guardians and their allies stood in stunned silence. The ominous force revealed by Nyxar promised a dire challenge, one that threatened to outstrip their current preparations.

The chapter ended with a palpable tension in the air, setting the stage for the next epic confrontation. The fate of the realms hung in the balance, with the true nature of Nyxar's threat yet to be fully revealed.

Milton Keynes UK
Ingram Content Group UK Ltd.
UKHW041122061224
452240UK00005B/442